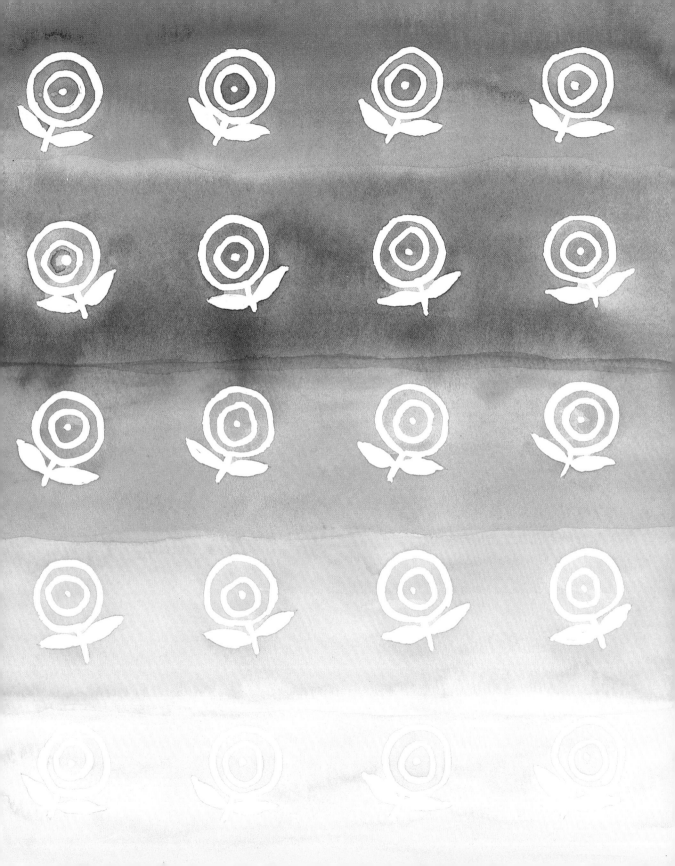

Other Picture Books by Kevin Henkes

A Weekend with Wendell
Chester's Way
Sheila Rae, the Brave

Jessica

by Kevin Henkes

HOLD ON TIGHT, JESSICA.

VIKING

VIKING

Published by the Penguin Group
27 Wrights Lane, London W8 5TZ, England
Viking Penguin Inc., 40 West 23rd Street, New York, New York 10010, USA
Penguin Books Australia Ltd, Ringwood, Victoria, Australia
Penguin Books Canada Ltd, 2801 John Street, Markham, Ontario, Canada L3R 1B4
Penguin Books (NZ) Ltd, 182–190 Wairau Road, Auckland 10, New Zealand

Penguin Books Ltd, Registered Offices: Harmondsworth, Middlesex, England

First published in the USA by Greenwillow Books 1989
First published in Great Britain by Viking 1990
1 3 5 7 9 10 8 6 4 2

Copyright © Kevin Henkes, 1989

Printed in Hong Kong

A CIP catalogue record for this book is available from the British Library

ISBN 0–670–83081–X

GOOD JUMP,
JESSICA!

For
Annie
and
Geri and Mac

WE'RE ALMOST THERE, JESSICA.

JESSICA IS MY
BEST FRIEND.

Ruthie Simms didn't have a dog.

She didn't have a cat,

or a brother,

or a sister.

But Jessica was the next best thing.

Jessica went wherever Ruthie went.

To the moon,

to the playground,

to Ruthie's grandma's
for the weekend.

"There is no Jessica,"
said Ruthie's parents.

But there was.

She ate with Ruthie,

looked at books with Ruthie,

and took turns
building towers
with Ruthie.

If Ruthie was angry, so was Jessica.

If Ruthie was sad,
Jessica was too.

And if Ruthie was glad,

Jessica felt exactly the same.

When Ruthie accidentally
spilled some juice,
she said, "Jessica did it,
and she's sorry."

When Ruthie's parents called
a babysitter because they
wanted to go to a film
one night, Ruthie said,
"Jessica has a stomach-ache
and wants you to stay at home."

And when Ruthie turned five, it was
Jessica's fifth birthday too.

"There is no Jessica,"

said Ruthie's parents.

But there was.

She went to bed
with Ruthie,

she got up with Ruthie,

and she stayed with Ruthie
all the time in between.

On the night before the first day of
nursery school, Ruthie's mother said,
"I think Jessica should stay at home tomorrow."
Ruthie's father said, "You'll meet a lot
of nice children. You can make new friends."

But Jessica went anyway.

COME ON, JESSICA.
IT'LL BE OKAY.

Jessica wanted to go home so badly that
Ruthie had to hold her hands and whisper
to her. When the teacher announced everyone's
name, Ruthie and Jessica weren't listening.

Jessica crawled through a tunnel with Ruthie,

she took a nap with Ruthie,

and she shared Ruthie's paintbrush during art.

When all the children lined up two by two
to march to the lavatory, Jessica was
right next to Ruthie.

A girl came up to Ruthie and stood by her side. "Can I be your partner?" she asked. Ruthie didn't know what to say.

"My name is Jessica," said the girl.

"It *is*?" said Ruthie.

The girl nodded.

"Mine's Ruthie," said Ruthie, smiling.

And they walked down the hallway hand in hand.

Ruthie Simms didn't have a dog.

She didn't have a cat,

or a brother,

or a sister.

But Jessica was even better.

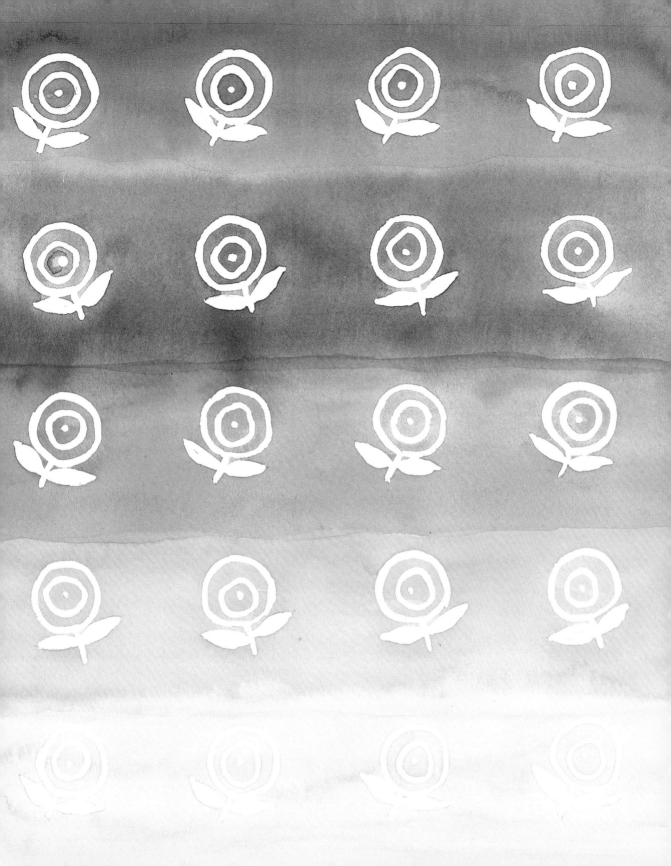